FORBIDDEN DESIRE

BOOK 2

PHOENIX SKYY

MIND FLOW PUBLISHING & PRODUCTION LLC

Additional copies of this book and others are available by mail.

Mind Flow Publishing & Production LLC

PO Box 48768 Cumberland, North Carolina 28331-8768

by visiting the website listed below.

Check the website for pricing.

www.mindflowpublishingproduction.com

Cover Design by RJ Creatives

Formatting by Carlette Whitlock

Copyright © 2023 Phoenix Skyy

Mind Flow Publishing & Production LLC

ISBN PAPERBACK 978-1-951271-77-0

ISBN EBOOK 978-1-951271-76-3

FORBIDDEN DESIRE

CONTENTS

DEDICATION

A special dedication to all of my family and my friends.

Thank you for being by my side.

Thank you to God for guiding my path

PROLOGUE

NETTE

This is what you're here for, I remind myself, gently tapping my pen to the rhythm of my racing heart. Helping people? I was an expert at that. I have a passion for saving others. Sitting down one-on-one and connecting with people is where I thrived the most. After all, had I not been the recipient of such kindness when my birth mother left me at the doorstep of a wolf shifter, would I even be here?

But right now? This is where my skills falter, and I wonder if I can even do this whole non-profit thing. Today I am delivering a presentation to our ever-growing audience of volunteers at Helping Hands. With over five hundred faces staring back at me with eager eyes, I couldn't seem to form what was so clearly written out before me.

Sucking in a deep breath, I detail the basics. "As most of you know, someone gifted us an extremely generous donation. The donor is an anonymous donor." My brothers in the background both stick their tongues out at me as if on cue. Okay, sure, I know the donor and yes, the money feels dirty to me, but in a world where the poor get poorer and people like our donors seem to climb to the top of our corpses? We take what we can get. But no one needs to know this. If they knew that self-righteous indignation would take root in their hearts. I know this because it still threatens to bloom on my own.

What they don't know won't hurt them. In fact, this money has already saved so many shifters' lives. Even the lives of non-shifters who are struggling in our neighborhood have benefited from this money.

"Because of this, we've been able to help so many people, and invest in ways that will continue to bring growing profits and donations to us. Of course, as you can see," I pause, and gesture around the small arena, "this has caused our numbers to grow. How great is that?" Everyone cheers and I imagine this is what a celebrity must feel like when they approach the stage to belt their latest hit. It's like a wild rush of endorphins takes over, and the fear melts away. I am proud. So. Fucking. Proud. And so grateful for all the lives we've been able to help.

"I am excited to announce that we are continuing our foster program for baby shifters. We will continue efforts to increase welfare for those struggling and provide counseling services. As most of you know, there are a lot of situations that plague our community, and poverty isn't the only issue. Some of us are struggling with our identities as shifters. Some of us even feel like monsters. And elite shifters condemning the rest of us do not help this."

The room is silent as the subject shifts. What I say next may rub some of them the wrong way, but it needs to be said.

"Most of you know, I am a panther. I am what should be rich. I should be elite. But I was abandoned as a newborn. I have been raised amongst you. I've been unwelcomed among the panthers and at times even among you." Some eyes fall downward, and I know my words have done what I intended them to. "I say this not to cause hurt, but accountability." I express myself gently and watch as those fallen eyes lift in understanding. "I will say this once and only once: everyone is welcome here. All shifters, and even the humans in our community, especially if they have ties to shifters. We will turn no one away."

The crowd cheers, and I see a shadowy figure enter the building. I can't quite make out who they are from here, but I can smell him from anywhere. Noah. I smile. Of course, he's in a hoodie and trying to hide himself. He would not be welcome here — the irony does not escape me but fills my soul with a deep ache. One day. One day it won't be like this, a voice in my mind whispers. I hope it is true.

I invite my brothers to come to deliver the gritty details about finances, schedules, buildings, and more.

I make my way to the shadow figure and slip my fingers through his. He squeezes them gently. "I can't stay long.

But I wanted to say I made sure my family stays out of this and we keep the donations flowing. Don't ask how."

His ominous message leaves me trembling. "Shh," he whispers. "It's nothing bad like that. Trust me. I have to go though. I'd kiss you, but we have an audience." He laughs.

Our attention is called back to my brother's declaring our meeting is about to end. "But first, we'd like to pay tribute to the woman who made this all happen." He points a controller at the screen behind him and our mother's face flashes on the screen as a sweet melody plays. "As many of you know, it is our mother who put that fire in us to help others. My sister Nette shared her story with all of you. They abandoned her as a cub. Especially back then, people frowned upon panther shifters. But our mom took her in without hesitation."

I squeeze Noah's hand, and he whispers, "Is your mom here?"

"I wish she was."

Just as I was saying this, my brother answers the same question. "Unfortunately, she is watching remotely from her bed at home." My other brother holds up his phone, displaying Mom on FaceTime to the entire audience. "Though she is recovering from her cancer, she is still unwell and a group this big? It's practically begging to catch an infection."

As the ceremony comes to a close, my body heats up. I've been craving Noah's body with such intensity; I am surprised I manage to sit through the entire ceremony without sneaking off. But before I can invite him over or run off with him, he slips away from me. "I have a meeting, but I'll talk to you later." And yet again I find him leaving me longing for more. Always more. Never enough. Why is he so far away lately?

I feel as if we reconciled despite all odds, but now I see him even less. My lips tremble with an unsaid goodbye, longing for an "I love you", but he's already out the door.

Chapter One

Noah

I screech my tires to a halt, almost slamming into the concrete wall in MidnightZ underground parking. "Shit," I growl. I can only imagine what the valet drivers glaring at me from their booths are thinking. But I didn't have time to deal with them. I didn't have time to even leave to begin with, but I wanted to show Nette my support.

Fuck. No one ever told me how fucking hard it was going to be sleeping with what the world considers my enemy. Or maybe it's the other way around. Maybe I am the enemy. Either way, our worlds hate each other, and I have to walk a tight line to appease everyone. Despite the massive falling out with my parents, I managed to keep my spot as CEO locked in place. My mother, surprisingly came to my defense and said to change things up, to toss me aside, and disown me would be a bad look for my father's political endeavors. Can't have that now, can we? Nobody likes scandal. Especially my family. Which is ironic, because they are the most scandalous of all.

I'd be lying if I said my father's neglect didn't haunt me. He couldn't possibly choose to reconcile his relationship with his son for just that. It fucking stung, but if I buried myself in work and Nette's body, I could forget it all.

"You're late," my father snaps as I barge through the doors of our latest meeting. Though he has technically stepped down as CEO, he is still attending far too many meetings than should be legal. No one says anything, of course. This is MidnightZ after all. Shifter-owned. Elite-owned. We don't abide by the rules. Unless you're a receptionist and you're caught breaking the slightest rule, my father is quick to remind you we are a company of integrity. As if the man knows what the word means.

"I had an errand to run," I answer dryly.

"I am sure you did." He flashes a knowing look.

The room watches us like the latest UFC fight, as if we are both about to pounce on each other — and let's face it, it's only a matter of time before we do. Especially if Dad keeps coming to these meetings. How much more of this bullshit does he expect me to take? I let out a low growl and took my seat. I am supposed to give a presentation, but I know whenever he is at a meeting, he takes over to where I can't get a word in edge-wise.

I allow my mind to dissociate as I already know the material. Deep down I know my authority is being un-dermined, and that his games are not ones I will play. I am staying in this business so I can be a light, as Nette would call it, but he is staying in it to prove a point — he is above everyone. Even me. If being with Nette taught me anything, it's that I don't want to be like my father. But I do have a position few others do, and from that position, I can bring about change. I can be a light in this company — and that can spread farther than I could from anywhere else. No one knows I'm still seeing Nette, but judging by my father's comments and that judgmental gaze, he still suspects it. And why wouldn't he? I'm still donating generously from the company credit card each month. I also made him vow not to lay a hand on her or her family - a vow that cannot be broken, according to pack law. The only law he must abide by. And should he dare break it, well... things would get nasty, and I'm not sure he is ready for that. Our pack is strong, but if his own son tried to fight him, the entire pack would question him.

Quite frankly, I know I am not ready for that kind of turmoil. Bringing my father down would not bring about a pleasant change.

My mind is a mess of family drama and the way Nette's hands trembled in mine. The way her eyes begged for me to stay — and goddamnit the way I wanted to. The way I wanted to stay and ravage her body as a congratulatory gift for all her hard work. *Soon*, I wish I could call out to her. Just a few more hours...

As I stand up to give my presentation, my father immediately cuts me off before I even switch to the second slide. I raise my brow. "Would you like to take over?" I snap, pleasantries falling away with my ever-growing frustration.

"Oh, now, Noah. Let your old man have one last go at the quarterly review, hm?"

I smile cordially, tossing him the Bluetooth clicker, and take my seat next to the other employees. A girl sitting beside me whispers, "Now we'll be here for three hours. You at least make it go by quickly."

I smile and whisper back. "I figure he'd do this. I ordered the team dinner set to arrive in about an hour. Should help us leave early." I wink.

My father coughs. "As I was saying, you can see that we haven't been performing well this year. Many of you know we have executed layoffs in many of our other departments. This is the only department that has been 'safe'. Much of that is because my son keeps advocating for you."

I smile. He's noticed. But he doesn't say it like a compliment, and I immediately sink as I feel his next words hit the room before he speaks to them. "I am laying off five people in this room." A threat. He doesn't say names, or when.

He continues with the meeting, all of us eerily silent until the secretary knocks on the door. "Food has been delivered."

"Can't say I have much of an appetite now," the girl next to me comments.

"Neither do I."

I pulled up to Nette's home and honk the horn several times. I would love to greet her and open the car door for her, but I can already feel all eyes on us. My skin crawls when I think of the people being unkind to her because she's been with me. Because she is a panther. I know why; I know people like my father have fostered this us versus them mentality, but Nette doesn't deserve to be the target.

"I thought you'd never show," Nette says, teasing and dripping wet. I hadn't even noticed it started raining! I feel even worse for not greeting her! Reaching my hand to her soaking locks, I trail my fingers across her jawline. She shivers.

"I'm sorry I ran off earlier without a proper goodbye."

"How sorry?"

"I'll make it up to you." I promise, before whispering a brief confession. "Things were intense at work,"

"Mm, how intense?" She questions. "Bet I can top it."

"Not sure about that." I pulled away, smirking at her breathless sigh. "You can top me, though."

As I hit the gas, pulling out of her neighborhood, Nette's delicate hands find their way to my lap. She applies pressure on my already growing length. "Dammit," I slam the brakes at the red light, which I swear appeared out of nowhere. "You're gonna make us crash, babe."

She smiles, clearly pleased with herself. "Then drive faster." She draws her hands back to her own lap before she inches up to her breasts, drawing teasing circles the way I wish I could.

"Within reason," I murmur a promise and hit the pedal once the light turns green.

I sneak glances as she continues to pleasure herself, her eyes on me as if my mere presence is all she needs to climax. A rugged moan escapes my own lips before I change lanes and take the back roads home. It'll be faster and with little traffic, I can sneak a touch here and there.

"No dessert until dinner," I murmur, pulling her hand back into my lap. She giggles and we both take turns teasing each other and teasing ourselves. As the stars sparkle in the distance, the further we get away from the bright city lights, I feel a deep knowing consume me: forever with Nette will never be enough.

CHAPTER TWO

NETTE

I could kick my own ass for teasing myself so much but goddammit was I *thirsty* as my brothers say. Keeping things low key with Noah means we don't see each other as much as I'd like which inherently means less sexy time together. I never considered myself one of "these" girls, but I suppose now that I've "had" it, had Noah and all his rough edges, it's all I craved. He is all I crave in so many ways. I knew no matter what happened with work, he'd find a way to make tonight work for us. After all, tonight was my big night with the non-profit. I deserved a treat. I spotted chocolates and more roses in the backseat, but we both know those could wait for later. Or during.

Why does he have to live so damned far away? I pause, teasing my own nipples. For a brief moment the answer gives me a taste of the reality I choose to ignore every time we are together: Because he is from an entirely different word. He is rich. You are poor. I shake the thought away, damning the distance — and this incessant rain. "I need you," I murmur.

"I know," Noah growls. "Stop."

I blink. "Did you just tell me to?"

"Stop. Dinner first, remember. Besides, I want to have my dessert too, you know?"

As if I couldn't come multiple times at the hands of this man. But I do as he says. When the light turns green and he hits the gas again, he commands me to continue.

"What?"

"You heard me. Touch yourself."

I eagerly do so, eyeing the bulge in his slacks. My fingers running down underneath my skirts and my panties to circle my clit. Our breaths are ragged, the raw energy of it all lighting us both on fire. He slams the break. "Stop."

I sigh, shivering with need. And so, our little game of red light and green light goes — a glorified game of edging

— until I simply can't take it anymore. I don't even realize we're at his place until the next thing I know he's at my door, lifting me up and carrying me into his place, my hips thrusting wildly with need. "Slow down, love," he whispers, but the command is still there clear as day.

"It's torture!" I whine.

"I know." Noah laughs, and as he punches in some numbers on the keypad to unlock his front door, I see his own fingers trembling with as much need as I feel.

With quick and graceful movements only a shifter can possess, Noah carries me to his room in a matter of seconds and tosses me onto his bed, pouncing on me. In the fury of need, my shirt is gone and I'm in nothing but my panties. His hand reaches over to his nightstand — I assume to grab a condom. Hadn't we gone over this? I'm on birth control … he knows this … but when I hear the slight rumble beside me, I realize he must've hit a switch. My jaw drops as what I always assumed was an ordinary wall in his room opens to reveal a chamber of sorts. Whips, ropes, sex toys that would put the local sex shop to shame, and a plethora of other items I don't even know what they are.

"Noah!" I gasped. I had seen some of this other stuff before, but this is either new or he was holding out on me.

"I wanted to experiment. Is that okay?"

"Hell yes," I declare enthusiastically. Sure, I have my limits — and he knows this — but some of those toys and the handcuffs look like they could be fun. Noah laughs as he makes his way to the little chamber. He hovers his hand over each item until I give a little nod. When he returns with a rope and a clit sucking device, I wonder if next time I'll be ready for more. Of course, we have plenty of rough and wild fun without any tools.

Noah takes the rope and ties me to his headboard. We had settled on a safe word weeks ago, and something in me stirs at the idea of our little game finally coming into play. "Tighter," I whisper, after he is done tying me into place. I am a shifter after all — even a tighter knot won't hold me, but he's being too gentle. He purrs and tightens the restraints.

Noah switches on the clit sucker and allows it to tease and taunt and please me as his mouth takes my breast in. My hips fervently rocking, begging for his cock, until he finally obliges and enters me. His shivering body causes my own body to quake with need. "Nette," he moans, his cock pulsating in me and I know it's been killing him to hold back, he's so close to the edge now. His lips hang heavily at my breasts and in this moment I feel powerful.

Whenever I am with Noah, I feel powerful. Invincible. The way a panther shifter *should* feel.

When he bites his lip it's over for me, I rock wildly against him until both of us are a sweaty mess moaning in an erotic chorus that is sure to put even the best adult creators to shame.

"Nette," he says breathlessly, rolling over and tossing the toy aside. "You're gonna be the death of me." Noah rolls back over and nuzzles into my breasts.

"I will protect you with my life," I say, a confession I wasn't ready to admit, but maybe it's the rush of dopamine coursing through my veins or a primal shifter truth, but it's him. He is my mate. I can feel that. I am bound to him, and he is bound to me. I would never let him die. I will always fight for him. For us. Forbidden love be damned.

"How was work?" I ask Noah gently. He had said things were intense, but I was so consumed by my own need in that moment. I wish our meetings didn't feel so rushed, so few and far between. I give my body and soul what we crave, but these precious moments of being there for each other are scarce.

He sighs. "Dad threatened to lay people from my department off."

"More people?"

"More? How did you know there were other layoffs? It hasn't hit the news yet and I didn't tell you…"

"They've been at the non-profit seeking help. He took away income from so many families and didn't even offer any kind of packages before dropping them. Some don't even have food and are behind on their mortgages."

"Oh," Noah replies, but his eyes are distant. The dopamine rush is fading, I feel so torn. I want to call him out on his lack of empathy, but I know this is delicate. We are delicate. If I say more, he'll know too much, and I can't betray my clients. Something in his annoyance that I know about what's happening at MidnightZ is unsettling. Am I not allowed to be privy to the horrible things his father is doing?

"I should go," I say, but it's only because I don't know what else to say. Or maybe it's because I want him to put his charming smile back in place and change the subject. But he doesn't even look up at me.

"Yeah," he agrees.

Wow. Okay. "I can request an Uber if you're too busy to give me a ride home."

"Yeah. I can request you one." He says absentmindedly. It feels like we're right back at square one, and I can feel my heart sinking. Is his behavior because I confessed how

I feel — in such a deep and raw way? Is he running away? Or maybe I read the room wrong...

My thoughts spin out of control, but I have to remind myself that we went through so much already. *If he didn't care, Nette, he wouldn't be here. It wouldn't be worth it.*

"They're just rounding the corner," Noah says, waving his phone and giving me a quick kiss on the cheek. "Did you get everything?"

"Mhm." I pull away to grab my purse.

I can't even bring myself to say goodbye.

He doesn't say it either.

The Universe must have a twisted sense of humor because as I'm still reeling from my conversation with Noah, I am faced with yet another layoff victim from MidnightZ. Her name is Lilly, and her blue eyes are filled with tears. "They paid us pennies for the work we did. I was a paid intern which meant I got minimum wage. They make it sound like the company is hurting so bad, meanwhile Noah Kahan is driving around in a Tesla and living in a mansion."

I cringe, feeling as if this woman can see right through me. As if somehow my own eyes scream that I was inside that very mansion last night, benefiting from this rich man in ways that would change how people in this community sees me. "We'll take care of you." Lilly reaches into her purse to show me her paystubs and bills. "Don't worry. I'll deal with the paperwork later. Let me just help you now."

She thinks my eagerness is kindness, and though I do want to help her, I also need to leave this building before my soul breaks.

My phone dings. *"We've found a possible match for your birth mother."* The text should bring me joy, but knowing what I do from Noah's father, I have no words.

I stumble my way to my car. "Nette! Nette! Hon, are you okay?"

I look up to see my mother. "No," I cry. "I am not okay." As she pulls me into her arms, I feel safe and all the confusion with Noah and my birth mom's situation fades.

It's just me and her. When I pull away, I look up at her worried eyes. "I need to tell you something."

"Of course."

"Let's go somewhere. That's not here."

"Sure! I was just gonna go grab lunch. Meet me at the cafe down the street?"

I nod.

"You're good to drive, right?"

I nod again. "Yes, mom. I'll be okay."

It takes less than a minute to get to the cafe. We both order our regulars and as we sip on our coffee, I offer her my phone and let her read the notification. I know she won't be upset, but I also don't have the words in me right now.

"Oh sweetie! That is wonderful!"

"Yeah but, the way... someone in the panther community talked about her... I figured she might be dead or something."

"Well, you won't know the truth until you find out. I think it's worth knowing. And you know, Nette, I won't be hurt by this. I think it's great."

CHAPTER THREE

NOAH

My hands curl into fists and my claws threaten to escape. My father is no longer in the middle of me and Nette, but it feels like he is. Am I just his puppet still? Once in my office, I slam my fist against a wall.

"What's eating you?" Tess asks, and I kick myself for not noticing she was in here. Why is she here?

"Didn't I fire you?" I seethe.

"You know your dad wouldn't allow that."

"So much for being CEO." I growl. I can't believe she has the audacity to still be here after what she did!

"Aw, well you're totally the CEO in my eyes." Her voice is toxic honey dripping into my already raw wounds from my not-actually-a-fight with Nette.

"Don't you have work to do?"

"Mm, I could do some work."

"Tessa," I warn. "Remember how this went down last time? I am in no mood for you and your little games. I am not your mate. I will never be your mate. My father can push his agenda all he wants but…"

She doesn't miss a beat, completely oblivious to the hatred boiling in my veins. "But you're with Nette?"

I blanch. "No. Obviously that will never work out. But if you were the last panther on the planet, I would never choose you. Not in any world, any reality."

"Ouch," she says, a smile dancing across her features. She truly is evil.

"What do you want Tessa?" I try again.

"Other than your cock," she enunciated the word hard with a need that would've once lured me straight into her pants. "Nothing. Well, I guess something. You father wanted me to let you know to let your little girlfriend know that she needs to stop digging into her past."

I frown. "What do you mean?"

"See! I knew it. She is your girlfriend." She twirls around, clearly proud of herself.

I open my mouth to argue with her, but she cuts me off. "Noah, if she keeps digging things will get bad for all shifters. I will not protect you and nor will your mother. You think that debacle from before was crazy? That was just an appetizer of what your father is capable of. You know that. Now, tell her to back the fuck off."

"Fine Whatever. Now leave," I command, and she obeys in a way that surprises me.

Once Tessa leaves, I allow myself a moment to growl into my hands and dig my nails into my desk — the giant claw marks will need to be repaired or covered before the next meeting. Not to mention the hole in the wall. At this rate, I need to hire a regular maintenance crew to clean up after my outbursts. I know I should call Nette to let her know about this latest warning, to see what Tessa means, but I am still aching at how things ended last night.

"I am so fucking stupid!" I sweep my half-shifted paws across the desk, knocking over paperwork and what I can only assume is a coffee Tessa left behind. How long was she waiting for me?

I hear rustling, and snap, "Leave me the hell alone!"

"I am so sorry, I... I was told to let you know... I... I can come back."

I look up to see a shaking intern. Shit. I thought it was Tessa. "I am so sorry you had to witness that. I thought you were someone else." I let out a low chuckle. "Today has Big Monday energy, if you know what I mean."

She laughs softly. "Unfortunately, I do. I um, your dad let me and a few of the other girls know today would be our last day."

"Wait. I didn't approve —"

"And I was told to let you know he wants to see you at noon."

This feels personal. "Lilly, is it?" I ask.

She nods.

"You're just an intern. Why would he include you in the layoffs?"

"I'm a paid intern."

I sigh. "Let me see what I can do."

She smiles weakly, and I can see in her eyes she doesn't believe I will try anything. She looks at me the way I look at my father. The way I am absolutely terrified Nette will one day look at me.

I cancel all of my meetings until noon. In fact, I leave the office completely without so much as a word, hopping into my Tesla and driving as fast as I legally can until I'm deep in the middle of nowhere, driving faster. It's not until I reach an isolated cabin my parents used to take me to as a kid that I am able to breathe. I don't often allow myself to shift outside of pack meetings and rituals — it's considered taboo and something other shifters like wolves do, something "dirty". It's primal and animalistic and though we have our rituals and pack laws and ceremonies... Panthers of the Midnight Shadows Pack is more human than most in that we blend. We use our power as a threat, we strive to be powerful yet 'normal'.

But sometimes the call is so deep, I don't give a fuck. I shed my human skin, my human worries, my humanity as my body bends and melts into an oversized panther. I can run faster than my Tesla can drive, and when I'm deep in the woods, I spot a wild animal. I don't think. I act. I launch at the deer and attack it. My paws are bloodied, I know this is why. This is why we don't shift alone. Still, I consume the beast before reluctantly making my way back to the cabin. My fur melts and gives way to my human skin once again.

I wipe the remaining blood on my lips, disgusted with myself. A brief thought presents itself - at least you're not hurting others. Not like your father. After all, the cruelty committed at the hand of my father is done when he is in his human form, surrounded by his loyal supporters. He has less humanity than even the cruelest beasts of the world.

My phone rings. I see Nette's name and my heart sinks. I walk into the cabin naked, hitting the ignore button, and hop in the shower.

That's the thing. When you know you're in the wrong, it's hard to face it. Especially when said "wrong" is your biggest fear.

I don't want to be like my father. I thought being part of MidnightZ, I would be able to help people, protect them from my father's tyrannical rule, but I can't. I'm just turning a blind eye. Because if I push too hard, I put Nette and her family at risk again — and I know that.

But Nette never really put the pieces together. She just trusted me when I said it was okay, that my father would leave her alone, that I could keep financing her non-profit, and we'd just have to keep our relationship a secret. If only it was that easy. I wanted to believe it too... but today was all the evidence I needed that there was no winning this battle.

After stepping out of the shower, I send Nette a text. "I need to see you." Without another word, I drop the location to the cabin.

Hours pass before there's a knock on the door. I sit my bourbon aside and stumble my way to the giant oak door. "You came," I say, my words slurring against my will. I must've drunk more than I realized.

"You called," she whispers. "Is everything okay? Where are we?"

"Oh man, are you in for a treat! Dad would flip if he knew YOU were here." I laugh and laugh and wait for Nette to join me, but she only squints her eyes at me. Fine — some people just can't take a joke! I loop my fingers through hers and guide her through the hall. I point out family pictures and she asks about the boy the one by my sports awards.

"Oh? Him? That's my mom's best friend's son. She couldn't take care of him. She got sick or something. He lived with us for a while."

"Um, Noah. You're drunk, aren't you?"

"What? Shifters can't get drunk!"

"I mean," she says, her voice tentative, "we can. And it looks like you drank the whole bar. So, it's safe to say you're drunk. You reek. You're acting strange."

"So what? I'm not allowed to have fun?"

"This isn't like you Noah. What's wrong? What happened?"

"Why does something have to happen for me to have fun? Jesus. Am I supposed to work all of the time? You know before I started fucking you, I was going to the club every night. I would get drunk all of the time." I shake my head. Bad idea. The room shakes with it, but it doesn't stop. "Dammit, Nette. I didn't call you over to fight. I wanted to apologize. I know I was a dick last night, but I am just so scared, and I don't know what to do. I am strong and a future alpha and all this shit, but you know what? I still don't know what I am doing."

Nette sighs. "Let's sit you down and get some water in you. And some coffee. We can talk, fight, fuck, whatever after your sober. But you will be sober."

I huff but let her lead me back to the living room. I see her look back at the picture of my childhood friend. Is she shocked I once had friends? Real friends? I drink the water Nette brings from the kitchen, and I can smell the coffee already brewing. "I'm going to grab some blankets. We can hash this out later. Right now, let's watch a movie while you sober up, hm?"

I nod, surprised by her kindness. Her firmness.

Deep down I know I don't deserve it.

She returns with a blanket and some DVDs she found upstairs. "Action or Rom-com?"

"You choose," I say gently.

"I've had quite enough action in my life today." Nette laughs, and it's warmer than the blankets, more soothing than anything I've ever known. "Rom-com it is."

We settle into our movie, Nette only leaving to bring me coffee and more water. I don't remember much of it, my eyes heavy and I doze off every now and again. When I wake up, the cloud has lifted. I'm only a little tipsy and the guilt of everything comes crashing into me.

"I am sorry you had to see me like this. Seems everyone is seeing me at my worst today."

Nette's cool hands caress my cheek. "You're hurting. We see this a lot back home. I work with a lot of addicts."

"I'm not an addict."

"I didn't say you were," she says calmly. "But you are using alcohol to cope with some pretty deep shit. And I know how quickly that can escalate into addiction. I'm still hurt by what you said. It's not okay. But I'm more hurt about what you didn't say while sober last night."

Here it comes...

"I feel like you're forgetting the purpose of going back to MidnightZ."

"And I feel like you forget how you almost died because of my father. Things like that don't just go away and get fixed with a nice little bow."

"I know that, but you said —"

"I said what I had to so you could feel safe. So, I could believe it too." I pause. "Tessa was in my office today."

Her eyes light up with horror. "What did she want?"

"My father wants to let you know to stop digging into your past. What does he mean, Nette?"

She sighs and reaches for her phone. "I think I might've found my birth mother."

Fuck. I was warned to keep her from digging. But now it's too late.

CHAPTER FOUR

NETTE

Noah reads the text, following the website it's from and reads even more, before handing my phone back to me. "That is wonderful news, but please be careful Nette. My father clearly knows we are still seeing each other and he's not happy about any of this."

"Let him do something," I snap. "I am tired of living in fear, Noah. You know that. I know you think I don't realize the severity of what happened, but the thing is I do. And what you don't know is I was waking up with nightmares. My mother has been doing her best to soothe her grown adult child. I am broken from everything that happened."

He flinches and I immediately tone down my anger. "Listen, I know this is impossible for both of us, but I think we're both diving in without a solid plan. You don't have a solid plan for bringing change to MidnightZ and are simply doing your best to keep people safe from your father's wrath. I know that. And I shouldn't be mad at you for the layoffs. You didn't lay anyone off. But you can't be mad at me for hurting with my people."

"You're right," Noah concedes. "I don't know what I am doing. We don't know what we are doing."

"And that's not a bad thing," I say, reaching to soothe him, but he pulls back. "Oh, Noah, come on. Get over the whole toxic masculinity trip, okay? Because of that. That is going to damage us."

"And what are we, Nette?"

"I thought I told you last night." I can see him racking his brain and I realize in that moment; he was so high from post-sex he must not have realized what I said. I punch him. "You idiot!"

"Ouch! What did I do?' He feigns pain, and I pounce on him, straddling him.

"Let's reenact it, shall we?" I whisper, my hips riding against him. I can feel his cock hard beneath his pants.

"I mean, I don't have my updated sex chamber here, but..." Noah flips me over, unbuttoning my pants. He pulls them down and my panties with them. "Guess my tongue will have to do," he murmurs before taking me into his mouth.

"Oh," I gasp. "Fuck this is even better," I moan, my hips slowly moving along with his lips and tongue. He slides a finger inside followed by two more, and my body quivers. He licks and nibbles until I collapse into myself beneath his lips.

With trembling hands, I reach for his bulging cock, eager to lead him into me. As he enters me, I'm already on the brink. My fingers shift and my nails dig into him, Noah lets out deep purr, as his hips thrust deeper into me.

"Don't stop," I plead. Somewhere my soul also pleads for him to never pull this crazy shit again. Everything melts together until I quake and feel him spasm on top of me.

"Someone left this for you," one of the volunteers says, handing me a black envelope with golden handwriting. I recognize the insignia which belongs to both Noah's pack and his company. The embarrassing goofy smile I feel in my soul must be reaching my face, because the volunteer giggles and says she hopes it's something good.

When she leaves, I grab a letter opener and gingerly slice the paper. Opening it, there is a handwritten note in what can only be described as expert calligraphy. I wonder if he had someone's help with this or is this, yet another skill Noah has mastered. "Meet me at this spot," it reads. Beneath the script are coordinates. I plug them into my GPS, grab my purse, and tell everyone I am taking the rest of the day off.

I follow Google Maps which takes me in all kinds of twists and turns until I'm far on the outskirts I begin to wonder if this is another elaborate trap from his father. My skin gets itchy with the thought, but when the maps tell me to turn left, I see him. Noah. My heart is filled with instant relief. He is holding a bouquet of flowers and the most loving eyes anyone could ever hope to behold them.

"Noah," I say, breathless. Behind him is a glorious meadow and a generous sized blanket. I wouldn't dare call the meal before us a picnic, as it looks to be catered by the finest restaurant in the city. He embraces me, murmuring sweet apologies.

"I need us," he whispers.

"Me too," I say.

I grab the bouquet he hands to me, and we take our seats on the blanket. "Let's eat, shall we? I have another surprise for us...."

"Do you now?" I wink.

"Not that. I mean, that too..." He laughs. "You'll see."

We are basking in the warmth of the sun as Noah continues, "This day is all about you. That's all I'll say."

His eyes sparkle as he says this, and I feel so foolish for doubting him. Of course, our relationship is going to be complicated — I know this, I've experienced my life at risk because of it. Staying in the thick of it for so long, it's almost like our relationship is in survival mode too. But this moment, just for now, I choose to let all of that go and enjoy the moment. I can practically feel myself drool as I take in the spread of delicious food Noah definitely had catered. "Oh, Noah, this is incredible! You really went above and beyond."

He starts to say something about money having its perks, before he shakes his head. "What I mean to say is," Noah corrects himself, his smile shining through and showing how truly genuine he is. He is trying so hard to be what we both expect him to be. "I wanted it to be special, Nette. Just for you." He pours us each a glass of wine that would probably pay my rent for the rest of the year and raises his glass in a toast. "To us, and to many more beautiful moments together."

Moments... Neither of us dares to think of anything bigger than that. Weeks... Months... Years... It's all too delicate.

Our glasses clink and our eyes lock with affection and admiration. We continue to enjoy the afternoon savoring the delectable treats, engaging in playful banter, and sharing stories of our childhood — learning more and more about each other. He laughs at the stories of my brothers and the chaos we would get into.

"I'm sure your mother loved every minute of it though," he comments, and I see a sadness cross his features. I know his parents wouldn't have been so kind had he done any of this as a child. I could only imagine their firm punishments. I squeeze his hand, deciding to share with him another silly memory to lighten the mood. It's strange how this simple day has deepened our connection with every shared laugh and gentle touch, far more than all the hours spent together at his place.

As the sun beings its descent, casting a golden glow over the meadow, Noah squeezes my shoulders, a surge of excitement flowing through us both. "It's time for the next surprise," he says before standing up, extending his hand to me. "Come with me, my love. I have something extraordinary to show you."

Intrigued with wide eyes, I place my hand in his. "Lead the way, Noah." I agree, "I can't wait to see what you have in store."

As we walk hand in hand through the swaying grass, our hearts beat in harmony with nature. "We have to shift to get there," he whispers.

I smirk. "So, we'll be naked upon our arrival."

"Is that where your mind always is?" he teases.

"As if yours isn't," I quip.

We strip of our clothes and place them safely in a nearby tree, before shedding this human skin of ours — and in turn all of my fears go with it. I am fearless. In control. I can hear his thoughts lead me, and it's a lot of climbing. A difficult trek our human forms could never complete without proper rock-climbing equipment... even then... it's too dangerous. I can see why he opted for this.

When we reach a secluded spot at the foot of a majestic mountain, Noah slips back into his human form, turning to face me, his eyes shining with anticipation. He kisses me, and I let out a deep purr. "This is one of my favorite places. The view from up there is breathtaking."

Slipping back into my human form, I make my way to the edge. My gaze followed his gesture, and my breath catches in my throat. The mountain we climbed is tall and grand, its peaks kissed by the fading sunlight. "Oh, Noah, it's absolutely stunning."

A mischievous smile plays on Noah's lips as he takes a step closer to me. "But wait, there's more. Are you ready for another surprise?"

Curiosity and excitement mingled in my veins as I nod eagerly.

With a surge of energy, Noah gracefully shifts once again into his panther form, his ebony coat glistening in the evening light. I am confused but taken aback by his beauty. Of course, I gasped, I have always been captivated by his panther form. He is beautiful, but what was his plan?

Inspired by his transformation, and assuming to accept this surprise, I too must let go of her human guise and embrace my panther self. My coat shimmers with a beautiful silver hue. We circle each other playfully, our shifter instincts guiding their movements. We run, leap, and chase one another, reveling in the freedom and exhilaration of their shared panther spirits.

The wind whispers through the surrounding trees, carrying our energy and the thrill of the moment. Our hearts beat in unison and our connection transcending the boundaries of human form. That's when I understand the surprise — we are truly in sync. Nothing is guarded anymore, and we understand each other perfectly.

As the moon ascends, casting a gentle glow over the landscape, Noah and I decide to shift back into their human bodies. We are back at the location where we placed our clothes, and slipping back into them we make our way back to the picnic. We stand facing each other, our eyes locking, and the bond between us stronger than ever. Who knew it was our human sides that kept us so far apart? So misunderstood?

My voice quivers with vulnerability as I spoke. "Noah, I love you, but sometimes I can't help but wonder if our differences will be our ruin. Can we truly make this work?"

Noah's expression softens, his eyes fill with determination and love. He takes my hands in his, his touch reassuring my soul. "Nette, I understand your doubts, but we've come so far together. I've done everything in my power to be different from my father, to be a better man. What more do you expect from me?"

I realize yet again, shifting into our human form, all of the understanding and connection we just experienced is fading. Tears well up in my eyes as I squeeze his hands. "It's not about expecting more from you, Noah. It's about my own fears and insecurities. I want us to have a future together, but I can't help but worry."

Noah's voice is consumed with emotion as he speaks, his words carrying the weight of his love. "Nette, our love is worth fighting for. We're stronger together, and we can face anything that comes our way. Let's embrace our differences and build a future based on trust, understanding, and unwavering support. We've already defied the odds, and I won't let anything stand in our way."

Relief floods my entire body, and I let out a breath I hadn't realized I was holding, so scared I had ruined our perfect night. I embrace Noah tightly. "You're right, Noah. I believe in us. Let's embrace our differences and face whatever challenges come our way. Our love is worth it."

We share a passionate kiss, our love and commitment sealing our future — I can feel it. Even if things don't work out, we are forever sealed. The mountain witnesses our unspoken mating ceremony of sorts, as our clothes fall to the earth and Noah lays my body down. The mountains standing tall as a symbol of our unwavering bond. With the night sky kissing our skin, his fingers graze gently across my thighs until reaching their destination. Circling my clit, I relish in the moment, feeling his hard cock against my leg. "Noah," I moan, reaching for his cock and leading him in, but he pulls away and instead first takes me into his mouth. My entire body on fire with each tantalizing lick.

"I told you," he whispers as he comes up from a breath. "This night is all about you, Nette... Every... Last... Moment... Of... It..."

Chapter Five

Noah

I smirk with each quiver and seductive moan I elicit from Nette's body. After she comes beneath my lips, I finally give her what she's been begging for. Sliding inside, she lets out the most delightful gasp and I am ready to continue to make each moment perfect. I know tonight won't take away our obstacles, but sometimes we need to be reminded about why we are fighting so hard to begin with. This is why. Nette is my why. Without her, I am afraid I would become the monster I am afraid of becoming.

The thought washes away as quickly as it came, as Nette's hips begin to ride frantically against me. "Nette," I growl. She digs her claws into my ass, pulling me deeper into her, and as I feel her spasm around me, I allow myself to come with her.

"Oh fuck, Nette." I moan, jerking a few more times before pulling out.

She takes a deep, shaky breath. "So, I know I said this before, but I don't think you understood. Noah, I want to be your mate. Officially. Like for real."

My mate? Words that ordinarily would cause me to bolt in the opposite direction from any woman have me frozen in delight and fear. "Nette... you know my family would never."

"Maybe if we go public, take all the criticism, that's a way around it all." I admire her hope, but I've seen darkness and I know the bitter truth. Hope is a foolish endeavor for the weak. We can't win with hope.

"I want to be your mate too," I confess. The words are strange on my lips. I'm not one to define anything, but of course I do. I wouldn't so much as fight a fly for any other woman before Nette. And for Nette, I took on my own father. My own ideologies. Everything... Of course, it's her.

It's always been her. I feel that in my bones. "Let's hold off on the public thing and make a plan. Like you said. We have to be strategic."

She nods, seemingly pleased with this response, before taking me into her mouth.

Nette and I reluctantly gather the remnants of our picnic. We laugh and tease each other, playfully jostling as we pack up the blanket, plates, and empty wine glasses. I am happy I achieved the desired result by having us shift, our bond having grown stronger without the complications of our human minds. Yet the bittersweet moment of parting tugs at my heart.

Loading the belongings into my car, we stand beside the trunk I just closed shut, facing each other. Nette's eyes held a mix of longing and contentment. I gently cup Nette's face, my thumb tracing my cheekbone.

"Come over tonight," I whisper, taken aback by the desire and eagerness in my voice. "We could continue the magic we started."

Nette's eyes sparkle with affection, but a hint of regret shadows her features. "I wish I could, Noah, but my mom needs my help with some things tonight, and tomorrow is going to be a busy day at Helping Hands."

I sigh, understanding the responsibilities that await her. It's her good heart and desire to help others that draws me to her. I lean in, my lips brushing against hers in a tender, lingering kiss. Her desire to say yes and stay is undeniable, but we both knew that even a brief separation couldn't dim the flame that burns between us. Things have been difficult, but I have to believe what we created tonight will carry us through.

"Alright," I whisper against her lips. "Take care, Nette. I'll be thinking of you."

Nette smiles softly, her fingertips caressing my cheek. "You too, Noah. Thank you for today. It was perfect."

With one last lingering look, we reluctantly parted ways, getting into our own cars. As we drive off into the fading light, the memory of the beauty of tonight lingers in our minds, promising a future filled with love and possibility.

We both get in our cars and drive our separate ways. It feels like we left so many questions unanswered and yet the greatest one of them all fills me with that dangerous hope. That feeling I hate. I do my best to shake it off, but I can't seem to wipe off my grin when I enter MidnightZ. It's an unholy hour but I still have so much work to do.

When I get there, my father immediately pulls me aside "Aren't you supposed to be traveling for campaigning?" I ask.

"Stop playing with me, boy. You missed our meeting yesterday. And you didn't return any of my calls today."

I laugh. "I had to get out. You miss meetings all of the time, Besides, you made your message clear. Tessa is a great little minion."

"She is not a minion. She is an obedient pack member."

"Sorry, I'm not. Actually, no I am not sorry. I am sick of your threats. You are supposed to be my father. I get that you're on a never-ending power trip, but you should be happy for me."

"Happy your back to fucking the enemy? Yeah, I know. And I know you were both at the family cabin. And I know you went to that little spot in the woods…"

"Are you following me?"

"Tessa is."

My jaw drops. "And how much did Tessa see?" And why didn't I sense her watching me? I frown, and realize I was drunk — and she must've left before Nette helped me get sober.

My father slams a folder in front of me. "This is all the information I have about Nette's birth family. Do with it what you will, but just know that not everything is what it seems."

I flip open the folder and my jaw drops. I know her mother. Her father too. They are my childhood best friend, Bo's parents. The Rowan family.

And they are just as vile as my father… "Why did they give her up?"

"The year Nette was born, some of the initiation tactics for joining the pack were… gruesome. Nette is the same age as Bo. You must realize what that means."

"She is his twin," I reply solemnly.

"Twins are a rarity. I tried to lead Nette off the trail of who she really was and who her parents really were… And you too. But you guys are stubborn and all these ancestry apps out there, well… She's going to find out soon if she doesn't back off. As pack leader, it is my duty to enforce these ancient laws. One such law is to instruct the parents of shifter twins to sacrifice the twins. Twins are considered an omen. Of course, sacrificing seemed too barbaric even for me… though you know how Bo's family is. They would've done it if I asked. Without a second thought."

I knew… I knew all too well…

"I said we could leave sacrifice open to interpretation. Bo lived with us for a while as a 'sacrifice' of time. They 'sacrificed' Nette to poverty. Son, I am in a deep battle with this family to maintain my position as Alpha and to ensure we do not go back to the old ways. I am a monster, I know, but I am not the monster you should be worried about.”

“What am I supposed to do with this information?” I ask, appalled.

“Do what you will,” my father says, walking away before I can ask any more questions.

Chapter Six

Nette

I stand at the center of the park, my heart pounding with anticipation. The stage is set for an epic water balloon fight, a playful and impactful way to raise awareness for our nonprofit organization, Helping Hands. My brothers stand beside me, armed with water balloons and mischievous grins.

A crowd has gathered, just as we intended, drawn in by the infectious energy and the promise of a fun-filled afternoon. Children and adults alike, all eager to participate in the charitable event, clutch their water balloons and donned their water-resistant attire. It is a sight that warmed my heart. This is the kind of public presence I seek to establish, a force that would protect my family, the foundation, and my relationship with Noah.

With a raised hand, I signal the start of the water balloon fight. The park erupts with cheers and laughter as balloons soar through the air, bursting on impact and drenching their targets. My brothers and I dart through the chaos, skillfully dodging the watery onslaught while retaliating with well-aimed throws. Our shifter abilities are surely aiding us in this battle.

As the fight intensifies, I can't help but feel a sense of pride. The community has come together, not just for a water balloon fight, but to support the cause I hold so dear. News cameras captured the excitement, and I found herself being approached for an interview.

"Nette, can you tell us about the changes Helping Hands is bringing to the community?" the reporter asks, holding a microphone to my face.

My smile widens as I take a moment to catch my breath. "Absolutely. Helping Hands is focused on creating a positive impact on our community. We're working to provide resources and support for families in need, to ensure that every child has a chance to thrive. It's about fostering a sense of unity and empowering individuals to make a difference. Today's event is just one example of how we can come together, have fun, and raise awareness for our cause."

The reporter nods, impressed by my passion. "It's truly inspiring to see the community rallying behind your mission. What do you hope to achieve in the future?"

My gaze sweeps across the park, taking in the joyous faces and the spirited water balloon fight still in full swing. "In the future, I hope to expand our reach, to touch more lives and make an even greater impact. Through Helping Hands, we aim to provide educational resources, healthcare access, and opportunities for personal and professional growth. We want to create a community that uplifts and supports one another, no matter the circumstances." I look at the camera fiercely — after all, those who know... know. We are shifters. And while I will help anyone in the community, it's the shifter community that inspired this movement. My mom's love for helping those less fortunate in our community of all types of shifters.

The interview concludes, and I return to the water balloon fight, my heart brimming with hope. I see my brothers, their laughter echoing through the air, and I join them in their playful pursuit. Water balloons burst around us once again, sending cascades of water in every direction.

As the fight comes to a close, my gaze falls on Noah, who has been observing the event from the sidelines. Our relationship is still such a delicate concept and reality. I can't help but feel a surge of gratitude for his unwavering support. This was our fight, our way of defying his father's influence and protecting our love. At least until we can figure out a more long-term solution. More eyes are on me, and my family know. A safety net of sorts. Sure, his father can burn the net down one way or another, but it's another obstacle at the very least.

Noah approaches, a proud and loving smile on his face. "You did amazing, Nette," he says, his voice filled with admiration. "The impact you're making, the changes you're bringing—it's incredible."

"I didn't know it was going to be such a big event. I was hoping. Did you call the news media? You know what. Never mind. I'm just glad you're here." I lean into him, my heart swelling with affection. "We're in this together, Noah. With Helping Hands and events like today, we can build a stronger foundation, not just for the community, but for us too. We won't let anyone tear us apart."

Noah's embrace wraps hard around me, our shared determination evident in his touch. "We've come this far, and we won't give up now. We'll face whatever challenges come our way, together. Remember the other night?"

I smile. Of course, I do. I am still riding high on that mountain top. As the sun dips below the horizon, casting a golden glow over the park, I know that we are not just raising awareness for Helping Hands, but also for our love and resilience. Even if it's only through the lens of his father's observations. I'm sure his father has one of his assistants here to report back to him. We will continue to fight for what we believe in, hand in hand, never allowing fear or doubt to overshadow our journey. And in that moment, surrounded by cheering crowds and the echoes of joy, I find solace in the knowledge that our love was stronger than any obstacle that lay ahead.

"Come to my place tonight?" he murmurs.

"I'll leave twenty minutes after you?"

"See you there." He winks.

"And where were you last night?" my brother sings as he walks past my office.

"Wouldn't you like to know!" I laugh. I know Noah says we have a hard road ahead of us, but knowing there is hope, it's blooming something in me that I was starting to lose. I welcome in our next client with a bright smile and eager eyes, until she takes a seat.

Mrs. Kahan. Noah's mother. "What are you doing here?" I blurt out.

"Hello to you too."

"I am so sorry. I mean, Mrs. Kahan, it is a pleasure to see you again. What may I help you with today?"

"I won't beat around the bush or take up too much of your time. I am a businesswoman much like yourself." She looks around at my office and I can see the disgust in her eyes indicating she doesn't approve of my "business".

"Go on," I say.

"I know you're still fucking my son."

I blink. "I wouldn't say —"

"And I am not here to scold you about it. I am here with a proposal."

I do my best to paint my features in neutrality, but I can't be sure if I am succeeding — I mean Mrs. Freaking Kahan is in my office and accused me of fucking her son! How can anyone remain neutral in that situation? I sneak a peek behind her shoulders, wondering if anyone else recognized her, and wishing she had shut the door behind her when she came in. The audacity of this family! No wonder Noah is such a mess. I have half a mind to say as much to her when she continues. "I would like for you to come work at MidnightZ. I would like your relationship to be public. I think it would do wonders for my husband's campaign, and given the right spin, we could do a lot of amazing work together."

"Did Noah talk to you?"

She frowns. "About what?"

I shake my head. "Never mind." I chew on the proposal and tell her I need to think about it.

"Don't take too much time." A warning, I note.

As soon as she slips out of my office, my brothers appear. "Is that who we think it was?" I can barely spill everything about it before they immediately shoot me down. "Don't you dare even think about it. After all that shit Noah put you through too! No way! We ain't letting our sister work for some sleazy company."

But maybe this is the answer to my hopes. The answer to help Noah make the changes he...we...want.

I hold the phone to my ear, the ringing of a pulse of anxiety that courses through me with each tone. "Answer," I plead to whatever invisible force will hear me.

"Nette," Noah's voice gets me. He sounds just as anxious as I feel!

"I saw your mom," I blurt. I'm doing that a lot today...

"Uh, yeah?"

"She was at my office."

"What? I am so sorry. I didn't know. What did she do? Are you okay?"

"She offered me a job."

"She what? Are you sure? Sometimes my mom speaks and —"

"I am sure," I cut him off. "Like a job with you. At MidnightZ. Should I, do it?"

"Well, we said we were gonna do things with a plan first, right? So, let's discuss the pros and cons."

"Okay. Con, I'd have to work with your dad. He's technically not the CEO but obviously he's there every day."

"Fair," Noah says. "Pro. We can have lunch together every day."

"Pro. We can make those changes we want. Maybe I can help some people get their jobs back..."

"Con. You might not be able to, and you'll feel really bad about it."

"Pro. I can make more money. Money is nice."

"Pro. We can fuck in my office."

"I think I'm sold," I say, laughing.

"I think I am too. When do you start?"

I laugh. "Your mom gave me her number. I guess I have to call her back?"

"Let me know how it goes... And Nette, be careful. I'm not sure why she's doing this, but if there is anything about my family, it's that they have ulterior motives. Always."

"I know."

It's been a hard day, and I haven't seen Noah since the water balloon fight. We've only talked on the phone about my new "job" at MidnightZ, which isn't officially starting until next week. I spent the entire week making sure everything would be handled at the non-profit as I start my new role. And Noah is busy too. I know he's working hard to fill his dad's shoes and try to ensure his dad actually lets him do just that, but there's been even more layoffs. Tensions are high at work with panthers pooling in for help. Panthers are the elite — why should they need, let alone deserve our help? At least that's what my brother's ask before I start to shift the tiniest bit, allowing my panther fur to be exposed. "Even among the elite there is a caste system of sorts, and when you are rejected by those at the top, no one wants you." I squirm under the weight of my own words. Unwanted. I finally found more information about my mother, but I haven't been able to do anything about it. Or maybe I have, and I've just been drowning myself in work. And Noah's body.

I decide to get some fresh air and think about what meeting my birth mother would mean for me. I make my way up the mountain, my footsteps light on the familiar path. The scent of pine fills the air, mingling with the anticipation that swirls within me. This place holds a secret, a special spot that Noah took me to just days ago. It symbolized a place where we could be ourselves, where our panther forms could roam freely. Perhaps it can be a sanctuary, a piece of solitude for just me too.

Or not. Because as I approach the clearing at the mountain top, my heart skips a beat. Something is off. There, standing amidst the tranquil beauty, is Tessa, Noah's ex-girlfriend. Or ex-fuck buddy. Whatever the hell she is. I scowl, my breath catching in my throat, and a mix of confusion and unease washes over me.

"What are you doing here?" I manage to say, my voice laced with surprise.

Tessa turns to face me, her expression a mixture of guilt and sadness. "I come here sometimes, Nette," she admits, her voice soft. "Noah used to bring me here. But I'm guessing he's passed on the torch if you're here now."

My heart sinks, a wave of emotions crashing over me. This place, our secret place, isn't so secret after all. Noah had shared it with Tessa before, a fact he never mentioned to me. The pang of betrayal gnaws at my heart, mingling with the lingering doubts that have haunted me. And then there's this strange version of Tessa standing before me. She is not quite the monster I've encountered all the time before.

"Why didn't he tell me?" I ask, my voice trembling with hurt, and I feel immediately embarrassed. I didn't mean to ask it out loud.

Tessa takes a step closer, her eyes filled with a mix of sympathy and regret. "I am sure he just didn't want to hurt you. He probably doesn't even know I still come here..." she explains. "Knowing him, he just wanted to keep this place special for the both of you. He wouldn't want it tainted with my memory..."

I take a deep breath, struggling to process the revelation. It's not just about the secret spot; it's about the trust I had placed in Noah, and the doubts that have been festering within me. The doubts that threaten to tear us apart.

"I used to not be such a bitch; you know?" Tessa confesses, her voice filled with a tinge of sorrow. Her words pull me from my heartache. "But this world changes you. Look, we become who we need to in order to survive, and Nette, be careful. If you want to be part of this pack, you will lose who you are."

Her words hang heavy in the air, echoing in the silence. I consider her warning, the weight of it settling on my shoulders. The world of shifters, politics, compromises—will it all chip away at who I am? Will I lose myself in the struggle to belong?

Tessa's gaze softens, her eyes filled with an empathy so incongruent with who I knew her to be. "Noah loves you, Nette," she says, her voice filled with sincerity. "And he's doing everything he can to break free from his father's influence, to be a better man. But you have to decide if you're willing to accept the sacrifices that come with being part of this pack."

A whirlwind of emotions sweeps through me—love, doubt, fear, and determination. I look out at the breathtaking view, the mountains stretching before me, and I find solace in the beauty that surrounds us.

"I love Noah," I say, my voice firm. "And I believe in him. But I also believe in myself. I won't let the challenges of this world erode who I am. I'll navigate the path with my own strength and integrity."

Tessa nods, a glimmer of admiration in her eyes. But just as soon as it appears it is gone and her cold, unkind features back in their place. "I hope you find the balance, Nette. Love can be a powerful force, but so is staying true to yourself. Be realistic. Trust me. The fall down hurts."

We stand there for a moment, two women connected by a shared love for the same man, both on our own paths of self-discovery. She may be looking at me with cruel eyes, but I can tell she is being sincere. Odd, I consider, but maybe that's just it. All of us are so layered that even the villains aren't what we think.

My first day at MidnightZ and everyone already hates me — and why shouldn't they? The company just laid off more employees than seems necessary even for a significant drop in revenue and they hire a new employee who just happens to be fucking the CEO. Yeah, I'd hate me too. Between boring HR training videos and snide comments in the lunchroom, I am beat as my shift is reaching its end.

"Hey, babe, come here." Noah calls out, and all eyes are on me again. I enter his office.

"Okay, everyone already hates me. Can you not call me babe in public?"

"But I thought my parents said we can be public?"

"Yeah, but we don't have to be so obnoxious about it at work..."

"Speaking of sex at work..."

"Noah!" I gasp.

He begins unbuttoning his shirt and without a second thought, I approach him with eager hands, but he steps aside before I can reach him. Patting an empty spot on his desk, Noah commands, "Take a seat, miss. I have some questions I'd like to ask you about your performance."

I oblige, sure to let my skirt ride up as high as it can.

"Good girl," he murmurs. "Now stay."

That's torture. Of course, he knows that. That's why he does this. With achingly slow movements, he removes his pants. I allow my fingers to roam my body while my eyes devour him. "You have a meeting in an hour," I remind him gently.

"I can cancel it."

"I think we can speed things up a bit though," I plead, as I lift my skirt up, my fingers reaching between my panties.

"Patience, pussycat."

I tilt my head. "Don't play with me here."

With shifter speed, Noah leaps down to the edge of the desk, his fingers delicately guiding me to remove my panties — which are instantly replaced by his lips. His tongue teases my clit with slow, firm circles as his hands grip my hip. Without even thinking, my ass scoots further to the edge, closer to his warm lips. Slow motions, matching his, I dance with his lips beneath me. Knocks on the door and phone calls sound like a distant buzzing, and I know I am losing track of time.

As his alarm starts to buzz, a gentle rhythm reminding him to prepare for his upcoming meeting, Noah picks up his speed and I follow along eagerly. I know he says this office is soundproof, but I can't help but feel the need to be quiet, but the closer I get the more impossible it is. "Oh," I moan, "Noah. Yes." I feel my claws shift out of my skin and dig into his desk before they retract back. Gripping a fistful of hair I push him deeper, as my body quakes and comes beneath him.

Standing up, Noah licks his lips. "You are delectable. Thank you for that snack. I should get to my meeting."

"Yeah," I agree, breathless. "You should do that."

"I'll see you tonight?"

"Mhm."

"Stay. As long as you need to ... recover." Noah winks, before slipping out of his office discreetly.

My body is still reeling from the love we made when I hear a ding on his computer. I roll my eyes. "I can't believe he doesn't lock this thing." I don't mean to look, but once I do it's too late. It's an iMessage from his father. "I need to know what you chose to do with the knowledge about Nette's parents. They will be attending next week's gala."

"What the actual fuck?"

Chapter Seven

Noah

Sometimes you know your enemy is setting you up for failure, but sometimes — you just don't fucking care. I've no doubt that my mother has a plan to bring Nette to work here at MidnightZ and maybe it will blow up in both of our faces, but the more visible we are together, the less likely they'll do anything to harm her and her family. And besides … maybe Mom and Dad had her best interest at heart in their own deeply twisted way. Looking at my phone, I see a text from my father pop up, "I need to know what you chose to do with the knowledge about Nette's parents. They will be attending next week's gala."

With a shaky breath and a decision, I know isn't mine to make, I respond: "I will keep this secret."

"Good. If you bring Nette to the gala, please be mindful of her interactions."

"Will do."

And sometimes I feel like I don't know what I am doing.

That none of us do.

And that's what causes the most pain and the most hurt in this world.

My heart sinks with guilt. Am I making the right choice? Or am I being selfish with Nette? Can my father truly be trusted?

"Noah."

I spin around with a bright smile to greet the reason I've been doing this all. The reason that I've dived headfirst into a forbidden romance, broke all the rules of my pack and my family. "Nette, sweetie. I'm just about to go to the meeting. What's wrong?"

"You know who my parents are. My real parents." It's not a question.

"What do you mean?" I ask, but by the redness in her eyes, I know it's too late.

"Tell me the truth."

I just told my father I wouldn't... Her parents are too dangerous... If she knew the truth that it was all some ancient pack ritual, that it wasn't a choice born out of trauma or need... "Can we talk about this later?" I ask, looking around, all eyes in the office on us.

"No. We will talk about this now, Noah."

"Nette. There's more to this than you know."

"The thing is Noah. You know more than I do. And you haven't said a single word to me." With a deep shaky breath. "You're just like them, aren't you? I keep fighting this idea. I keep trying to tell myself that you're different and that everything we've been through proves that, but this trauma bonding bullshit... This isn't it. You were so keen for me to agree to your mother's job proposal... Is there more to that too? You know what," I pause and take a moment to breathe, holding my hand in the hair to silence him. "Don't answer that."

"Nette," I growl. "There is so much you don't understand about panther pack laws, our rules, and why we are the way we are. You do not know the power you possess. You do not know the truth of who you are. And trust me, you do not want to know where you came from. I am not the only one who came from monsters."

"Noah..."

"If you don't trust me, then leave. I know there are so many unknowns here." I wave my hand around, an entire audience now forming around us. "If you want to be part of my world, if you want to be my mate like you said, then you need to learn what it means to be a panther. You may come from a different world, Nette. But you can't be part of mine if all you want to do is hate every aspect of it. I have tried and tried to stop the layoffs at MidnightZ. I have tried to be a better man. A better shifter. A worthy CEO and a worthy soon-to-be Alpha."

"Please..."

"My family is dangerous. Panthers are dangerous. Everyone in this room knows that. We are predators, Nette. You are a predator. You may have been raised by a pack of wolves in your little humble abode, but you are a panther. We have the power to create and destroy. Some of us lean more one way than the other. We are the most ancient breed of shifters, and we abide by ancient and primal laws. You don't know anything about those. I am trying to bring change, Nette. We were doing so good..."

"Are you done?" she asks.

I shake my head. "No." I rake my hands through my hair. "But I have a meeting to attend, and we've already given our audience here quite the show."

"I wasn't the one yelling."

"Nette. We will talk later. You know this is complex. It's not that simple. Trust me on this and please trust that I am sorry, but I am hurting and confused too. I will make this right, but I can't right now." I step closer, and when she flinches, I step back. "I'll see you later. Nette, I... I love you."

The meeting is a blur of figures and promises. I know we might not deliver on one hundred percent, but the client eats it up, and I land another partner to be under the MidnightZ umbrella. I should be proud, but all I can hear is Nette's voice and see the disappointment in her eyes.

"That was intense," Tessa purrs in my ear.

"Why are you here?"

"When will you stop asking that?"

"When you stop existing?" I snap. "Also, I thought you'd get the idea that Nette and I are official. You need to back off. We somewhat have my family's blessing..." Even if I'm still uncertain as to why. Sure, it may be good for my dad's campaign. Maybe they really aren't entirely bad guys. Nette could be a great asset to the company... There are a lot of less than evil reasons, but after the shit Dad pulled... after all that's happened, of course Nette doesn't trust me. Or my family. And to know I was lying to her... I could kick myself in the ass for yelling at her. So publicly too.

As if reading my thoughts, Tessa continues, "Are you sure about that? Cause that looked like a breakup to me."

"Then I have nothing to keep me from being rogue."

"Oh, Noah Don't be so dramatic."

"Dramatic? You're literally kind of a murderer."

"Only a little bit." She winks. "Whatever, look, go chase after your girl. I'll wrap things up around here."

I blink. "Is this some kind of trick?"

"Let's just say your mother had an inspiring conversation with me."

More vague messages. Sometimes I wonder if perhaps I knew the truth, more than just my childhood indoctrination into this pack, this life... maybe I could understand. Maybe I would know what choices to make.

"Anniversary or apology?" the cashier asks.

"Apology," I answer. "That obvious?"

"This many roses and that much chocolate? You're either celebrating or you made a big mistake."

"Well, hopefully she gives me a chance to explain." I swipe my Amex and wait for the receipt to print.

"Best of luck."

"Thanks."

Peeking at my cell phone, I gloss over the endless notifications from my parents — of course they heard about the fight, they're worried about Nette's birth parents being revealed, and what this will mean for the pack. I wish I knew the entire truth of what this would mean, but I can only imagine. I remember the nights with Bo when he lived with us, the way he woke up with nightmares of the abuse his parents enacted upon him. Forcing him to hunt for his food — Bo was the first person who took me hunting outside of a pack ritual. We caught a coyote together. His family has long sought to bring my family down, to take over as leaders of the pack ... "purists" was a word that was thrown around a lot when speaking of them.

I pull up to Nette's place, and I see her mother, brothers, and her sitting on the porch. Her brothers immediately greet me before I made it to the steps. "You don't belong here," Lawrence warns me.

"I need to explain." I say, waving the roses and chocolate.

"Man, you think flowers are the way to say, "sorry I'm a rich douchebag who hid the identity of your birth parents from you?"

My anger is like knives coursing through me, begging me to shift. To deck this fool who knows absolutely nothing in the face. *He is Nette's brother. You can't hit him. That will only make things worse.*

"Nette," I call out. "Can we please talk? If after I explain everything to you and you still want to walk away, I will let you go, and I will never come back."

Chapter Eight

Nette

"Oh honey," Mom says, "give the boy a chance to explain himself. I sure wish you would've told me you two were still a thing sooner!"

"We were keeping it a secret because of his family…"

"Exactly! His family sounds complicated. I mean, quite frankly it sounds like he's done a great deal to keep you safe from them. And well, the rest of us too."

"He's a panther…"

"So are you," Mom snaps. "Did I raise you to be ashamed of yourself? Of where you come from?"

"No but —"

"No buts. I worked tirelessly for everyone in this home to love themselves no matter where they came from. Especially you. Your blood may be that of a privileged line of shifters, and they may have a reputation that is unsettling at times, but Nette... You of all people should know you can't judge someone by their reputation. You gave him a chance for a reason. You're not one to give up on people."

I nod. "I know, I know. I just." I flail my hands. "Okay, okay. No excuses. I get it." I holler at my brothers to back off.

With defeated looks and what I can only imagine are hushed whispers filled with threats, the two walk away.

"Noah," I greet him and instantly everything I was holding in bubbles over. Tears fill my eyes much to my disappointment.

"Oh, Nette. Can we talk somewhere a bit more..."

"Private?" I could already see the neighbors peeking out of their blinds. This truly was quite the show. Between MidnightZ and my neighbors, this city will be full of gossip. Everyone will know we are official... that is if we make it through this.

"Let's go." He hands me the flowers and chocolates, freeing his hand to wrap around my waist and lead me to his car.

Once inside, I let the tears fall. "Dammit."

"I second that," he agrees. "Damn this whole mess."

He switches on the car and begins driving. "I am sorry for how I handled everything. I should've told you sooner and when you confronted me, I was the one making a scene. Not you. I've already issued a public email with HR and PR to be sent to all employees. Should you decide to come back to work at MidnightZ, which my mother so adamantly said she hopes you do, there will be no awkward or strange contentions."

I blink. "What about your father? He can't be happy about any of this."

"He isn't." Noah laughs. "He was livid when he found out my mom hired you. He's insane, Nette, I know, but would you believe it if I said I think he has his reasons."

"I believe you might believe that. He's your father."

"And I both hate and love the man dearly," Noah confesses. "I want you to learn more about my pack. About where you come from. Even if we don't talk after this, you deserve to know far more than I've told you. You deserve to be welcomed as one of our own, should you decide to resign your membership with the Lone City Wanderers."

"I... I don't know what to say, Noah."

"It comes as no surprise after everything that being part of Midnight Shadows Pack and especially the inner circle of the elite is a lot like being part of the mafia, for lack of a better comparison. My family is corrupt. They manipulate to get their way. They kill to get their way. They climbed their way to the top and they didn't do so ethically."

"I figured."

"My father's entrance into human politics, blending the lines between shifter laws, politics, and owning a corrupt business... Well, let's just say he is a powerful and terrifying man."

"To say the least," I concede.

"But it seems he did have a reason for fighting to keep you and me apart. It wasn't solely your ideologies. And what he told you about your family before wasn't the entire truth. You remember when we were at the cabin?"

"Yeah..." Where is this going?

"That boy in the pictures with me? His name is Bo. Well, he is... I didn't know until today... but he is your brother. He was my best friend growing up... but things with his family got dark. I mean, they were always kind of dark. His parents were always feuding with mine."

"My brother..." I chew on the words. Noah takes his hands off the wheel — and I realize we have parked and are sitting still. My body is entirely outside of itself. I have a brother.

"Your twin, actually..."

A twin! "But... that would mean..."

I want to slap Noah's face but not because I am mad at him anymore — because I want the pained expression in his eyes to disappear. No. Don't say it. I assumed my mother was a victim and that I was likely only part panther.

"Twins in pack law are considered a bad omen. Ancient law commands them to be sacrificed. Being the purist they are, your parents were eager to sacrifice both of you in the traditional sense of the word."

I gape. This is too much. "Noah..." I breathe. I want to tell him to stop. I don't need to know anymore, but the words are stuck in my throat, tied into a massive knot, anchoring me into the car's seat.

"My father, being the Alpha, advocated for a looser interpretation of the law. Because males are more sought after and a rarity in the panther line, they decided to sacrifice Bo to live with my family for a set amount of time when he reached a certain age. As for you, they sacrificed you to 'live in poverty'."

"Oh my god..."

"I am so sorry, Nette. I couldn't tell you this. I mean, how can I tell you this?"

"I understand," I answer robotically.

"Nette. Look at me."

"I can't," I confess.

Noah breathes. "I understand."

"It's too much."

"Well, your parents are going to be at the gala tomorrow. Word is already spreading that there is an orphan panther working at MidnightZ. One who 'made a scene' about her birth parents in the office."

"You want me to meet them."

"No. But I want you to know they probably know you know they exist. This opens up a can of worms not just for you but for my family as well."

"And I care why?" I snap.

"Because I care about you. I don't know what they'll do, Nette. You're in this now, whether you like it or not. I understand if you never want to talk to me again, but remember how you said I need to act strategically?"

I nod. "I need to play my cards right."

"They're unpredictable, Nette. If you think my family is bad, well... no offense, but your birth family is batshit. Even my father is scared of them."

Mr. Kahan scared of someone? Chills course down my spine. "I'll go."

"I'll text you the details."

"I'll go with you." I continue, looking Noah in the eyes finally.

"Oh...Okay. Well, let's get you home, Nette. It's been a long night and —"

"I want to go home with you," I whisper, my voice aching with longing.

Noah smiles and laughs - it's a melodic sound that is something between relief and his own desire.

"Well then, your wish is my command."

All of my anger and hurt transforms itself into raw sexual desire the moment we step into Noah's house. A house I once judged him for — and I realize that even in our happiest moments, I was still holding onto such resentment. He must've felt so torn, stuck between me and his family.

"Let's play with some more toys, hm?"

"Are you sure?" Noah asks, his cock pressing against me through his jeans as he nibbles on my ear.

"More than sure."

Noah scoops me up and carries me to his room, switching open his chamber, and this time I let out a little moan of need when his hand hovers over the whip. Arching my hips in the air, my ass exposed, I whimper with need. So much need. With a quick jerk a hot ache spreads across my ass cheeks, delightful and painful at the same time.

With a few more whips while I pleasure myself, teasing my own body, Noah tosses it aside. "I need you," he growls before pouncing on me and guiding his cock inside.

"Fuck," I gasp.

With him entering me from behind, Noah has full access to hold my breasts as he pushes my body harder against him. My ass wildly rocks against his cock, as his fingers trail from my breast to my clit. With small, fervent circles, I let out a low moan. My nails dig deep into his headboard, as his teeth graze my shoulder and back.

"I'm so close," I plead, and the pain and pleasure mingle together and heighten every moment in a way I never thought possible. "Fuck me harder," I beg, thrusting my ass up against his cock.

"Dammit, Nette," Noah moans. His finger still circling my clit as he thrusts deep in me, our bodies, a frenzy of speed only a shifter would possess. "I'm gonna come," he whispers.

I feel his cock tighten within me and in that moment, I join him, our bodies spasm together.

Chapter Nine

Noah

Midnight Gala is a grand occasion that comes along once a year. All panther shifters and other elite members of society attend. It is a time for aspiring members of the pack to prove themselves. Those seeking to break into this world I grew up in to make their name known. From dancing, shifter rituals, political and pack agreements, and a feast that would put any cooking or local chefs show to shame.

It is also a time to vote on the Alpha of the pack. My father rarely has anyone vote against him retaining his position, but of course, every year the Rowan family does. And this time, their long-lost daughter will be making a return. With me. We are walking a precarious line, but it's too late to turn back. Nette is in too deep... and all my secrets are making their way to the surface.

And tonight? Tonight, I will announce that she is my mate. I've let my mother in on this little scheme of mine — well, not so much a scheme, but a way to safely officiate our relationship. I am protecting both of us from my father and Nette's parents.

Nette's hands dig deep into mine as she eagerly awaits this announcement. We do our best to focus on the food and avoid the darker parts of the gathering, but when it's time to vote for Alpha, her parents stand up. I hadn't had yet to introduce her to them — they were sure to avoid both of us.

"I would like to invoke pack law 82," Mr. Rowan says.

The room is filled with gasps and growls.

"What is pack law 82?" Nette asks.

"It is a battle to the death. It's an ancient law. No one heeds it or invokes it. When you have a qualm with a member of the pack, law 82 states that you can resolve the issue by battling. And it is acceptable if the battle results in death."

"What?"

"It has to occur in 10 minutes. That's how long the fight can last. It's truly archaic…"

"With whom?" My father calls out, his eyes filled with fear and fury.

"You. Mr. Kahan."

"What?" I snap. "You can't do this."

"I can and I will. If we start cherry picking which pack laws we will follow, then our entire system is corrupt." He looks over at Nette. "Unless you want to take your father's place. After all, should your father lose this battle, well, I'd be the new Alpha. Not you."

"Noah," Nette cries.

I hush her. "Very well," I call out, so the entire crowd can hear me. "But we are not monsters. We will have this battle in a week's time. Allow each of us to get our affairs in order."

"Son!" my mother and father cry out together.

"I volunteer on behalf of my father to solve your dispute per your invocation of law 82."

"Noah... What is happening?" Nette's eyes are wild, and for the first time I instantly regret dragging her into this.

I kiss her lips and do my best to wear a fake smile. "We'll share our happy news after this silly little fight."

ACKNOWLEDGEMENTS

A special "Thank You" to all of you who take the time to read my work.

With Love

Phoenix Skyy

Also By

Phoenix Skyy

Diva Crazy in Love

Because of You

Forbidden Series (1 - 3)

www.ingramcontent.com/pod-product-compliance
Lightning Source LLC
Chambersburg PA
CBHW051812050726
47598CB00006B/2530